P9-CSB-652

For my parents

Text and illustration copyright © 2006 by Shaun Tan • All rights reserved.
Published by Arthur A. Levine Books, an imprint of Scholastic Inc.,
Publishers since 1920, by agreement with Lothian Books, Melbourne, Australia.
SCHOLASTIC and the LANTERN LOGO are trademarks and/or registered
trademarks of Scholastic Inc. No part of this publication may be reproduced,
stored in a retrieval system, or transmitted in any form or by any means, electronic,
mechanical, photocopying, recording, or otherwise, without written permission
of the publisher. For information regarding permission, write to Scholastic Inc.,
Attention: Permissions Department, 557 Broadway, New York, NY 10012.

INSPECTION

Library of Congress Cataloging-in-Publication Data
Tan, Shaun. The arrival / by Shaun Tan. — 1st ed.
p. cm. Summary: In this wordless graphic novel, a
man leaves his homeland and sets off for a new
country, where he must build a new life for himself
and his family. ISBN 13: 978-0-439-89529-3
ISBN 10: 0-439-89529-4 — [1. Emigration and
immigration — Fiction. 2. Immigrants — Fiction. 3.
Stories without words. 4. Cartoons and comics.] I.
Title. PZ7.T16123Ar 2007 [Fic]—dc22 2006021706
25   18/0 First edition,
October 2007   Printed in Malaysia   108
Scholastic Inc., 557 Broadway, New York, NY 10012.

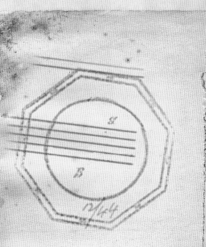

✳ THE ARRIVAL ✳

Shaun Tan

ARTHUR A. LEVINE BOOKS

AN IMPRINT OF SCHOLASTIC INC.

I

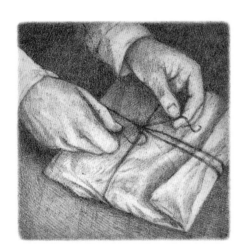  

II

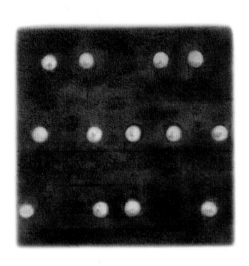

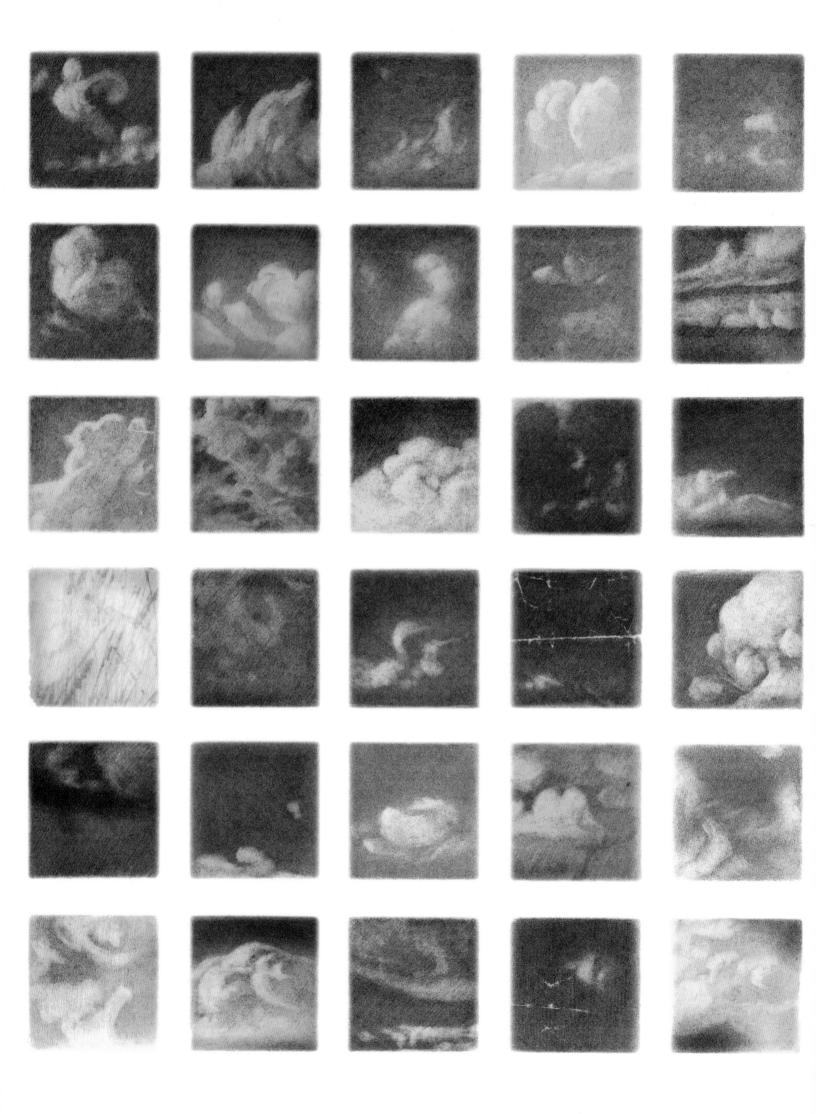

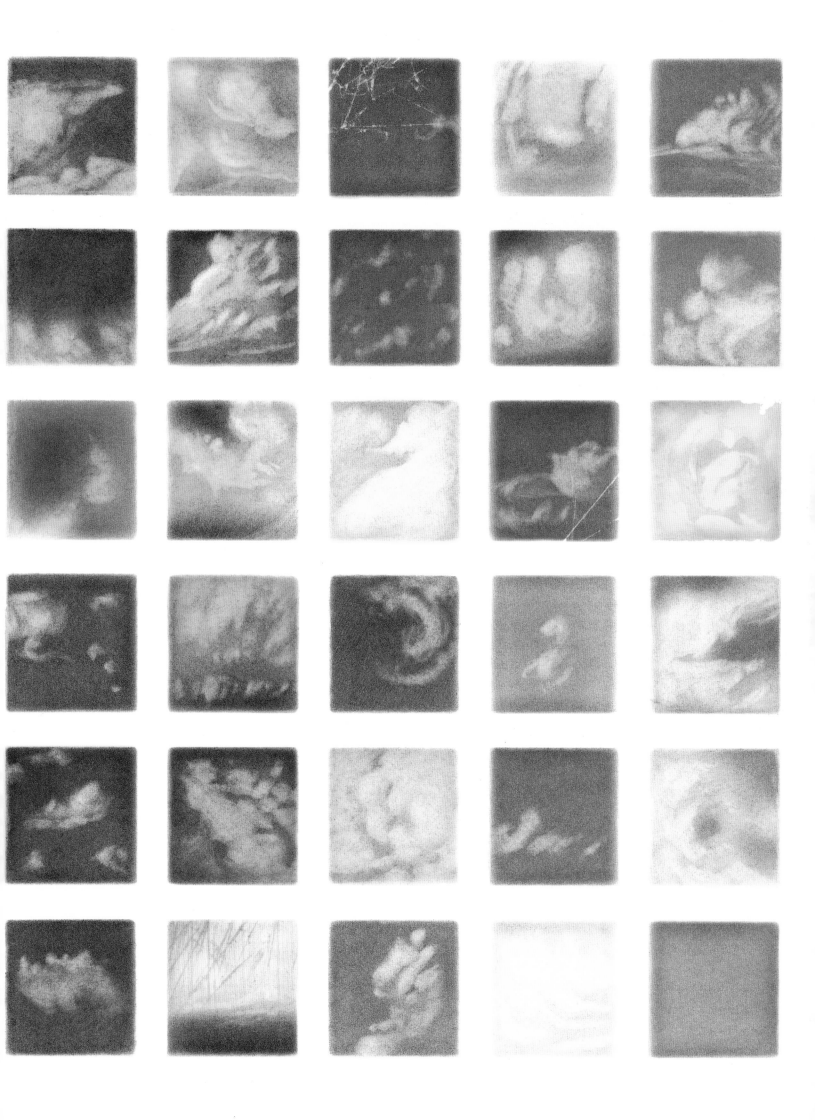

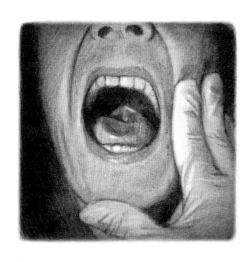  

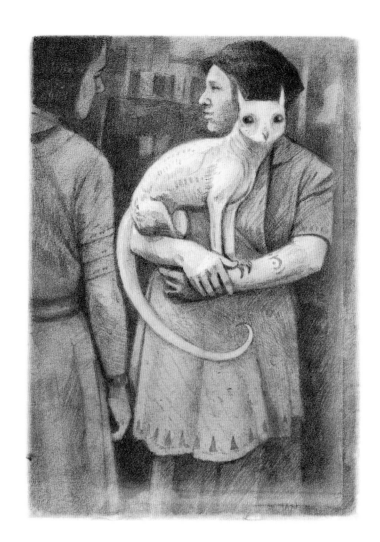

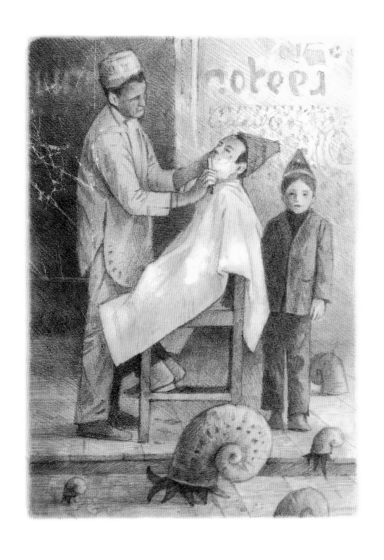

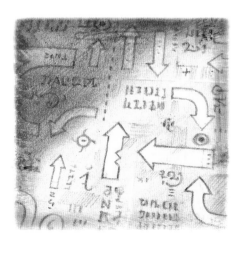

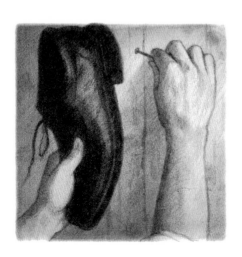

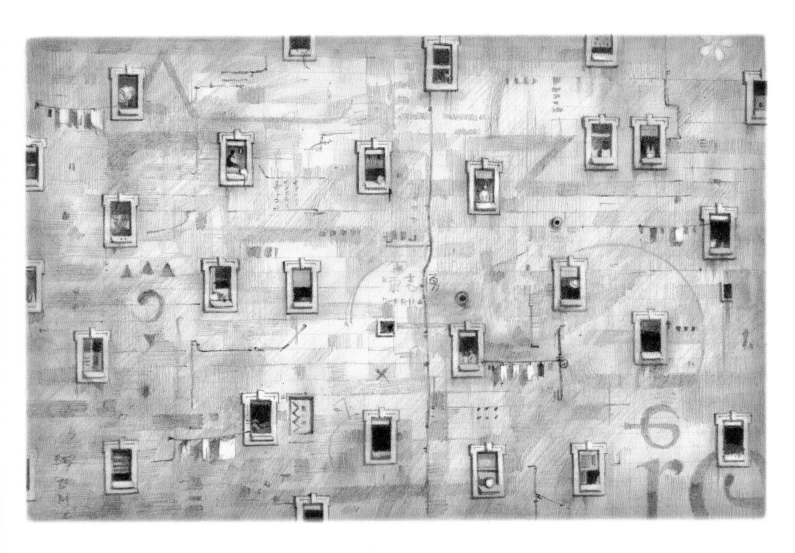

III

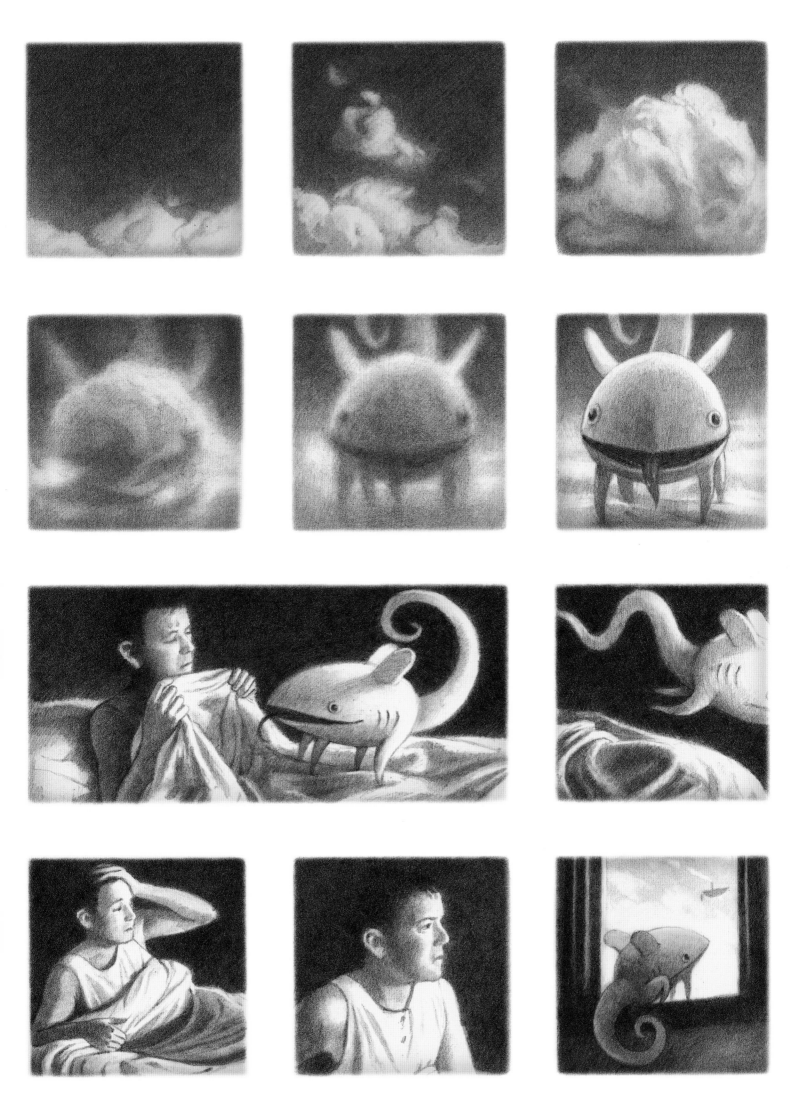

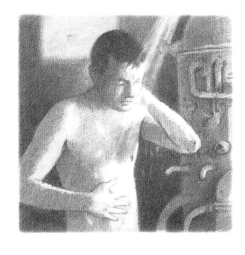  

IV

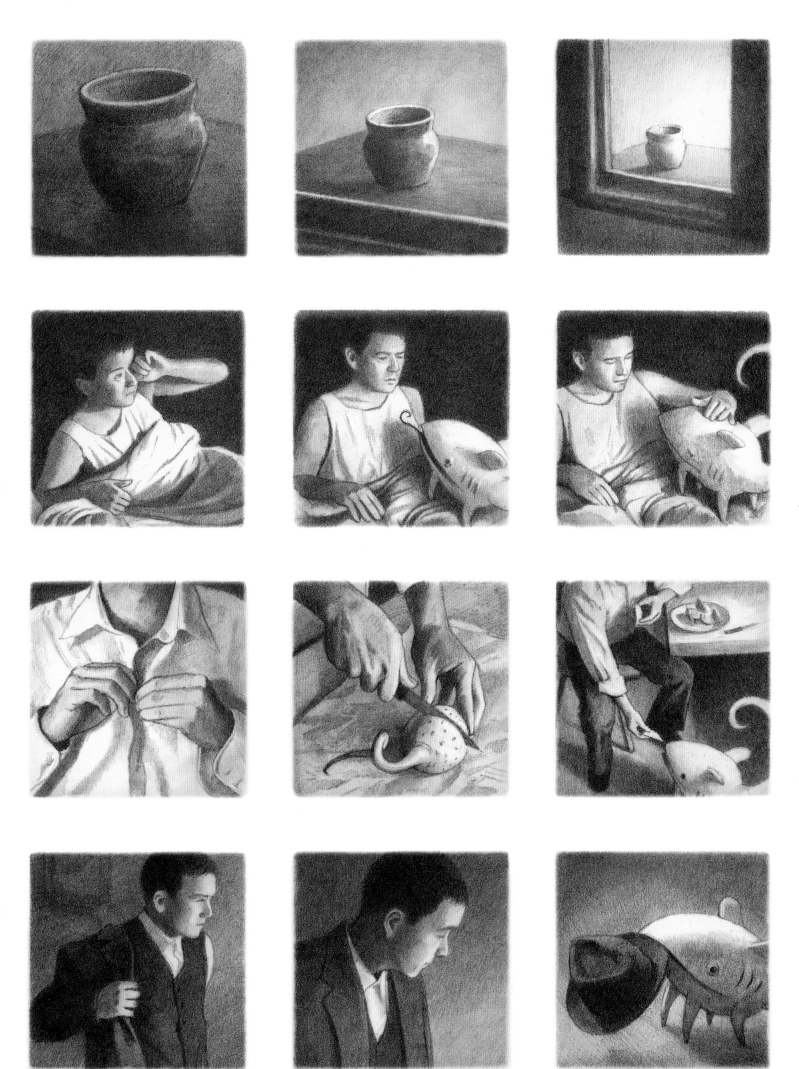

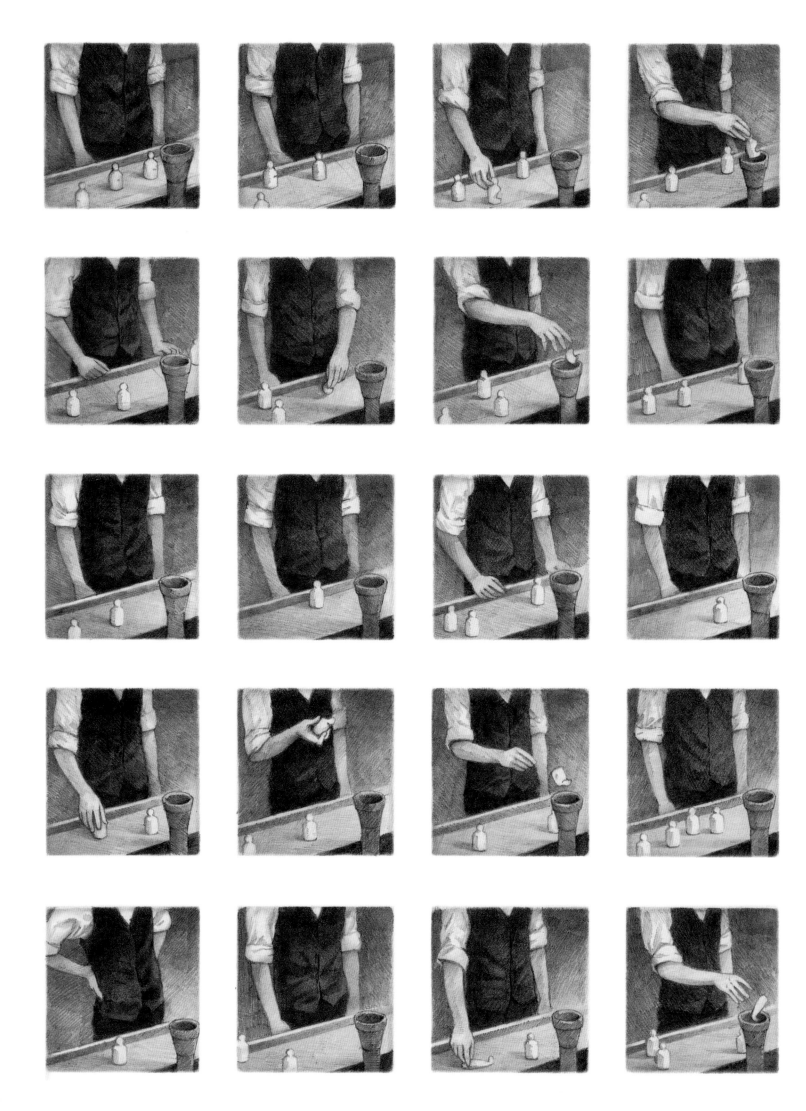

V

  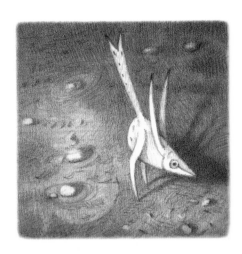

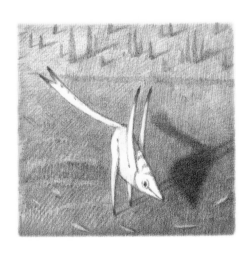  

VI

ARTIST'S NOTE

I am grateful to the following people for their assistance during the four years of research, development, and drawing that went into this book: my parents Bing and Christine Tan, Paul Tan, Helen Chamberlin, Sophie Byrne, Amanda Verschuren, Susan Marie, Rachel Marie, Simon Clarke, Deanna Cooney, Sophia Witte and Sarah Weaving, Zacharie Evers, Philip Evers and Kirsten Schweder, David Yeates and Kathryn Robinson, Karen Kennedy and the Bold Park Community School, Jeremy Reston, Nick Stathopoulos, the Ruffo family, everyone at the Fremantle Children's Literature Centre, Christobel Bennett at Subiaco Museum, Will Lauria, Peter Lothian, Tina Denham, Anna Dalziel and all the staff at Lothian Books for their ongoing faith — and patience! My greatest appreciation goes of course to my partner, Inari Kiuru, for all her support, advice, and encouragement. Special thanks go to Diego the parrot for inspiring most of the creatures in this book.

Thanks also to the Australia Council, The State Library of Western Australia, Inglewood Public Library, the Town of Vincent Public Library, and the National Maritime Museum in Sydney. Much of this book was inspired by anecdotal stories told by migrants of many different countries and historical periods, including my father who came to Western Australia from Malaysia in 1960. Two important references were *The Immigrants* by Wendy Lowenstein and Morag Loh (Hyland House 1977), and *Tales from a Suitcase* by Will Davies and Andrea Dal Bosco (Lothian Books 2001) — many thanks to all those who described their journeys and impressions in these books. The drawing of migrants on a ship pays homage to a painting by Tom Roberts, *Going South*, 1886, at the National Gallery of Victoria, Melbourne. Other visual references and inspirations include a 1912 photograph of a newsboy announcing the *Titanic* sinking, picture postcards of New York from the turn of the century, photographs of street scenes from post-war Europe, Vittorio De Sica's 1948 film *The Bicycle Thief*, and Gustave Doré's engraving *Over London by Rail* circa 1870. Several drawings of immigrant processing, passport pictures, and the "arrival hall" are based on photographs taken at Ellis Island, New York, from 1892 to 1954, many of which can be found in the collection of the Ellis Island Immigration Museum. For further comment, please visit www.shauntan.net